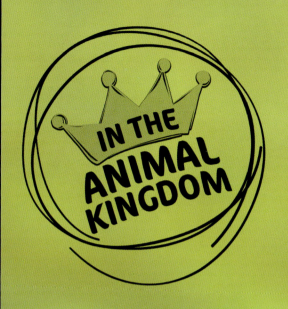

IN THE
ANIMAL
KINGDOM

AMPHIBIANS LIVE ON LAND AND IN WATER

By Sarah Ridley

WAYLAND
www.waylandbooks.co.uk

First published in papaerback in
Great Britain in 2021 by Wayland

Copyright © Hodder and Stoughton,
2019

Editor: Sarah Peutrill
Designer: Lisa Peacock

ISBN: 978 1 5263 0935 8

Printed and bound in China

Wayland, an imprint of
Hachette Children's Group
Part of Hodder and Stoughton
Carmelite House
50 Victoria Embankment
London EC4Y 0DZ
An Hachette UK Company
www.hachette.co.uk
www.hachettechildrens.co.uk

Picture credits: Kurit Afshen/Shutterstock: front cover. CreativeNature_nl/
istockphoto: 6l. Federico Crovetto/Shutterstock: 11b. Stephen Dalton/
Nature PL: 16b, 22b. Dirk Ercken/Shutterstock: 1, 6br, 15b.
Fablok/Shutterstock: 9t. Michael & Patricia Fogden/Minden Pictures/FLPA:
14, 18. Daniel Heuclin/Nature PL: 19. Vitalli Hulai/Shutterstock: 9b.
Hilary Jeffkins/Nature PL: 15t. Rene Krekels, NIS/Minden Pictures/FLPA:
11t. Lapis2380/Shutterstock: 17b. Fabio Liverani/Nature PL: 3b, 21b.
Edvard Mizsel/Shutterstock: 12t. MYN/Tim Hunt/Nature PL: 13.
Nature Production/Nature PL: 20. Jason Ondreicka/istockphoto: 7t.
Pete Oxford/Nature PL: 2b, 7b. Dr Morley Reed/Shutterstock: 23b.
Jason Steel/Shutterstock: 17t. Kim Taylor/Nature PL: 12b.
David Tipling/Nature PL: 10. Tremor Photography/Shutterstock: 2t, 8.
Stephane Vitzhum/Biosphoto/FLPA: 21t. Martin Voeller/Shutterstock:
3t, 23t. Pan Xunbin/Shutterstock: 16t. Bildagentur Zoonar GmbH/
Shutterstock: 22t.

CONTENTS

The animal kingdom

Scientists sort all living things on Earth into five huge groups called kingdoms. All the animals belong in the animal kingdom.

The animal kingdom is divided into two very large groups. The invertebrates are animals without a backbone and the vertebrates are animals with a backbone.

INVERTEBRATES

ANIMAL KINGDOM

Then we divide the vertebrates up again, into five large groups: fish, amphibians, reptiles, birds and mammals.

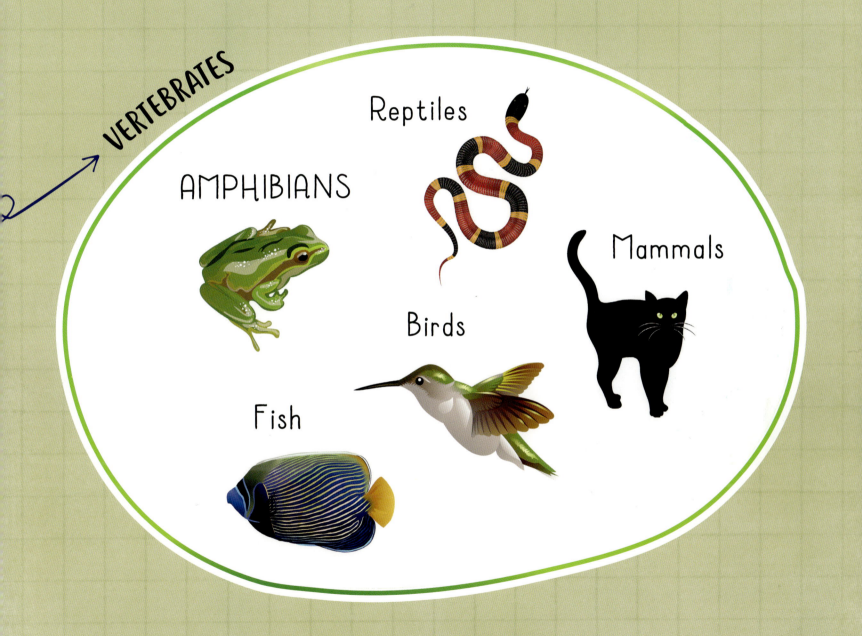

Read on to find out what makes an animal an amphibian.

Amphibians live on land and in water

Most amphibians live on land and in fresh water at different times in their lives. This frog was once a tadpole living in water.

Adult newts live near ponds, lakes and marshes, where they hunt for food.

Salamanders live in damp places or in water.

Red salamander

There are between 6,000 and 7,000 different types, or species, of amphibian.

Some caecilians burrow through damp leaves or soil in rainforests but others live in water.

Amphibians need wet skin

An amphibian must keep its skin wet or moist or it will dry out and die.

Adult amphibians breathe using lungs and through their thin, moist skin.

Salamander

How can you tell a frog and toad apart?

Frog

Toad

One way is to look at their skin. A frog's skin is wetter and less bumpy than a toad's.

Unlike amphibians, reptiles have watertight skin.

Amphibians lay eggs

Almost all amphibians lay soft, jelly-like eggs in water. These frogs are surrounded by their eggs, which are called frogspawn.

Frogspawn

Usually, a female newt fixes each of her eggs to an underwater plant. The tadpole develops inside the egg.

Newt egg

This type of salamander lives in caves in Italy and France. The female lays her eggs in a damp place and protects them while they develop.

Which other animals lay eggs?

Most amphibians do not look after their young

Most amphibian parents mate, lay lots of eggs and then leave. But some amphibians are different.

The male Darwin's frog keeps his tadpoles safe in his throat sac until they have turned into frogs.

Throat sac

Froglet

This caecilian mother feeds her babies a special liquid and allows them to eat her fatty skin. She regrows it every three days.

Tadpoles

When the eggs of the three-striped poison dart frog hatch, the father carries his tadpoles to rain pools in treetop plants.

Most amphibians have four legs

Most amphibians move on four legs. Frogs have long back legs that they use to hop, jump, climb and swim.

The Wallace's flying frog uses its webbed feet to glide from tree to tree.

Toads crawl along on four legs.

An axolotl is a type of salamander. It swims using its tail and lives in water all its life.

Caecilians have no legs

Caecilians look like earthworms and have no legs. Like all amphibians, caecilians are cold-blooded. This means their bodies become the same temperature as the air around them.

This caecilian is burrowing through leaves in a rainforest.

Caecilians spend most of their lives underground. They are almost blind and are most active at night.

This caecilian is eating an earthworm.

Caecilians have a backbone. Do earthworms have a backbone?

Amphibians eat other animals

Almost all amphibians eat other animals such as bugs, slugs, worms, spiders, tadpoles, eggs and small fish.

Toads shoot out their sticky tongue to grab insects.

On land, newts hunt insects, slugs and worms. In water, they eat insects and other minibeasts, larvae and eggs, including frogspawn.

This newt is eating frogspawn.

A frog has caught a dragonfly. When it blinks, its eyeballs press into its mouth and help push the dragonfly down its throat.

Amphibians live across the world

Amphibians live on all continents except for Antarctica.

The rain frog of South Africa sleeps underground for months, coming out about twice a year when it rains.

Amphibians that live in colder places hibernate over winter. The photographer lifted a log to find these sleepy newts.

Giant salamanders live in rivers and streams in China and Japan. They can live for fifty years or more.

In the Amazon rainforest, a male tree frog calls to females by pulling air into its throat sac.

The smallest known amphibian in the world is a tiny frog that is just this long: 7 mm.

⊢⊣

Glossary

adult An animal that has grown to full size.

backbone A row of small bones that are connected together to form the spine.

breathe Take in air and breathe it out again.

gills Parts of the body of an animal, such as a tadpole or a fish, that absorb oxygen from water, allowing the animal to breathe.

hatch To come out of an egg.

hibernate When an animal slows its body right down so that it can sleep through winter.

insect An animal with six legs and a body divided into three parts.

larvae The young of certain animals, especially insects, which hatch out of eggs and will develop into adults.

mate When a male and female animal of the same species join together to produce young.

moist Slightly wet.

rainforests Thick forests in warm parts of the world that have a lot of rain.

watertight Does not allow water to get in or out.

young Another name for animal babies.

Index